D0436997

7

6

5

4

3

2

1

peg + cat

THE CAMP PROBLEM

A LEVEL 2 READER

JENNIFER OXLEY
+ BILLY ARONSON

CANDLEWICK
ENTERTAINMENT

This book is based on the TV series *Peg + Cat*.
Peg + Cat is produced by The Fred Rogers Company.
Created by Jennifer Oxley and Billy Aronson.
The Camp Problem is based on a television script
by Meryl Schumacher.
Art assets assembled by Sarika Matthew.
The PBS KIDS logo is a registered mark of the Public
Broadcasting Service and is used with permission.

pbskids.org/peg

Copyright © 2018 by Feline Features, LLC
Text by Andrea Cascardi

All rights reserved. No part of this book
may be reproduced, transmitted,
or stored in an information retrieval system
in any form or by any means, graphic,
electronic, or mechanical, including photocopying,
taping, and recording, without
prior written permission from the publisher.

First edition 2018

Library of Congress Catalog Card Number pending
ISBN 978-0-7636-9921-5 (hardcover)
ISBN 978-0-7636-9922-2 (paperback)

17 18 19 20 21 22 CCP 10 9 8 7 6 5 4 3 2 1

Printed in Shenzhen, Guangdong, China

This book was typeset in OPTITypewriter.
The illustrations were created digitally.

Candlewick Entertainment
an imprint of Candlewick Press
99 Dover Street
Somerville, Massachusetts 02144

visit us at www.candlewick.com

Contents

Chapter 1
CAMP NINIWAWA

Peg, Cat, and Ninja Girl Aki were going to Camp Niniwawa. So was Peg's space creature friend Richard. He was nervous.

"You will love camp," said Peg.

"We'll play all day," said Aki.

Cat said, "Our counselor, Jesse, is a Teen."

"Yo! Newest Gopher," said Jesse.

"What did he call me?" asked Richard.

Peg drew a gopher. "The gopher is a cool little animal. Gophers is the name of our bunk. A bunk is like a team."

The team curled their fingers to make the gopher signal.

The Gophers sang their bunk cheer: "Gophers, we always go for it!"

"I don't feel like cheering or playing. I feel like going home," said Richard.

"Richard can't go home.

We've got a BIG PROBLEM," said

Peg.

"There's more than cheers
and sports at Niniwawa," said
Jesse. "Tell him, Ramone."

Ramone was the arts and
crafts counselor. He showed
Richard how to build with
ice-pop sticks.

Richard made a ladder.

It was red-red-blue-blue-
red-red-blue-blue from bottom to
top. "I love when things repeat
in the same order!" he said.

"Richard is all about
patterns," said Cat. "This
ladder goes first thing, first
thing, second thing, second
thing."

"Like Ni-ni-wa-wa," said
Richard.

Everyone cheered. "Niniwawa,
Niniwawa, woo, woo, woo!"

Richard was a happy Gopher.

Problem solved! The problem
was solved!

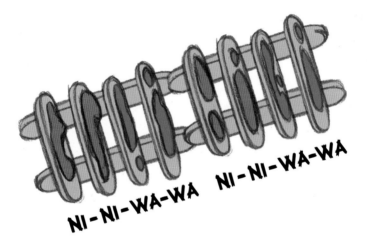

NI-NI-WA-WA NI-NI-WA-WA

Chapter 2
BATTLE OF THE BUNKS

The Raccoons bunk marched in
and sang their cheer.

"Hey, Jesse," said Tessa,
their counselor. "Check out my
super bunk, the Raccoons." Tessa
made the raccoon signal by
making circles around her eyes
with her hands.

"They are really loud," said
Jesse.

"I know," said Tessa.
"Raccoons are fierce! Raccoons
rock!"

"Gophers go! Gophers are
quick!" replied Jesse.

Peg said, "We shouldn't
think only about winning."

"Peg is right. That's why the Gophers are totally not competitive," said Jesse.

"The Raccoons are way less competitive than the Gophers," said Tessa.

"The Gophers are the least competitive bunk ever," said Jesse.

"Let's settle this with a super big contest," said Tessa.

"A battle of the bunks!" said Jesse.

"Whoever gets to one
hundred points first wins,"
said Tessa.

Peg said, "But it's not
always about winning."

"You can get five points
for being a good sport," said
Jesse.

"Okay!" said Peg.

The Raccoons did a warm-up drill with a very big rock. They were very strong.

"We have to compete against those guys?" The Gophers were scared.

"We Gophers have a REALLY BIG PROBLEM!" they said.

Chapter 3

THE CONTESTS

The first contest was watermelon eating.

The Gophers ate and ate. But the Raccoons had a secret weapon: Big Mouth could eat many watermelons all by himself.

The Raccoons got ten points.

The bunks shook hands, showing good sportsmanship. So the Gophers got five points.

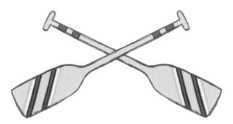

Next was rowing. The Raccoons won. They got ten points. The Gophers got five more for being good sports.

Then came the egg-carrying race. They each had to run while carrying an egg in a spoon--and trying not to drop it! The Gophers broke all of their eggs. The Raccoons got ten more points. The Gophers got five for good sportsmanship.

The Raccoons won every contest.

Tessa counted all of the Raccoons' points. "The Raccoons got ten points for winning the first game, plus ten points for winning the second game."

Richard said, "Please count faster!"

Peg said, "Counting by tens is just like counting by ones, but with a zero on the end."

She counted. "Ten, twenty, thirty, forty, fifty, sixty, seventy, eighty. And you just got ten more, so that's ninety."

"Meanwhile, the Gophers got five. And five more." Jesse counted on his fingers. "That's ten. And five more is..."

"Don't they teach counting
by fives in high school?" asked
Cat.

"I was absent that day,"
said Jesse.

5 10 15 20 25 30 35 4(

"It's kind of like counting
by tens. Except instead of
always ending in zero, it goes
five, zero, five, zero, five,
zero, five, zero."

"So we've got five, ten,
fifteen, twenty, twenty-five,
thirty, thirty-five, forty,"
counted the Gophers. "And five
more gives us forty-five."

"The Raccoons' ninety is way ahead of our forty-five!" said Peg.

"How did that happen?" asked Jesse.

"We keep getting five. They keep getting ten," said Peg.

"Ten is twice as much as five, so their lead keeps growing! If they win one more game, they will get to one hundred. They will win the battle of the bunks!"

Chapter 4

RESCUE

The Gophers hoped the last
contest would be ninja flips or
arts and crafts.

No! It was tug-of-war!

"We don't have a chance,"
said Richard.

"Gophers don't run and hide.
Gophers are ready to GO!" the
Gophers cheered.

The tug-of-war began. The
Raccoons tugged very hard.
The Gophers landed in the mud.
When the rope went slack, the
Raccoons went flying. They flew
backward so fast that they got
stuck in a tree!

Tessa said, "Gophers, we need you. If you get the Raccoons down, you can have five points for sportsmanship and ten points for coming to the rescue. And ten more and ten more and ten more and ten more."

"Of course we'll help," said Peg.

Cat took an ice pop out of the cooler. "That's it, you genius Gopher!" said Peg.

"Richard, remember the ladder you made out of ice-pop sticks?" Peg asked.

"This one?" Richard held up the ladder.

"Can you make a bigger one
to get the Raccoons down?"
asked Peg.

"I'm seeing full-size red
and blue steps in the Niniwawa
pattern," said Richard.

"These logs would be
perfect!" said Aki.

The Gophers stacked logs to
make a ladder all the way up to
the Raccoons.

"By using patterns, we're totally rescuing the Raccoons," said Peg.

"You totally earned those points," said Tessa.

"We didn't do it for the points," said Peg.

"Points are nice sometimes, am I right?" said Cat.

"If you insist," said Peg.

She added the points to the scoreboard.

"Forty-five plus five for good sportsmanship makes fifty. And ten for rescuing the Raccoons, and ten more and ten more and ten more and ten more makes sixty, seventy, eighty, ninety, one hundred!"

"The Gophers win the battle of the bunks!" said Jesse.

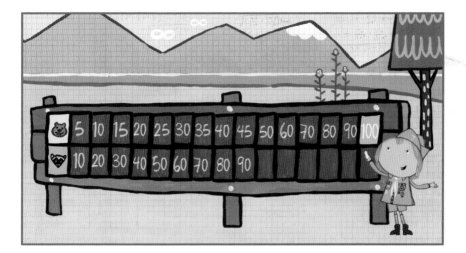

"And the Raccoons are safe and sound on the ground," said Tessa.

"Math rocks!" said Peg.

And so, the problem was solved. The bunks solved the problem. PROBLEM SOLVED!